FOCUS ON THE FAMILY

THE IMAGINATION STATION

Trouble on the Orphan Train

BOOK 18

MARIANNE HERING
COVER ILLUSTRATED BY DAVID HOHN
INTERIOR ILLUSTRATED BY
DAVID HOHN AND AMIT TAYAL

TYNDALE

FOCUS ON THE FAMILY • ADVENTURES IN ODYSSEY®
TYNDALE HOUSE PUBLISHERS, INC. • CAROL STREAM, ILLINOIS

In honor of Charles Loring Brace (1826–1890),
visionary for the Children's Aid Society,
and Rev. Thomas H. Hagerty, a modest man
who rode the Little Rock Express 7
on January 31, 1874

Trouble on the Orphan Train

© 2016 Focus on the Family. All rights reserved.

A Focus on the Family book published by Tyndale House Publishers, Inc., Carol Stream, Illinois 60188.

Focus on the Family and Adventures in Odyssey, and the accompanying logos and designs, are federally registered trademarks, and The Imagination Station is a federally registered trademark of Focus on the Family, 8605 Explorer Drive, Colorado Springs, CO 80920.

TYNDALE and Tyndale's quill logo are registered trademarks of Tyndale House Publishers, Inc.

Cover design by Michael Heath | Magnus Creative

Cover illustration and interior illustrations on pages iv, 2, and 5 copyright © David Hohn. All rights reserved.

All other interior illustrations copyright © Amit Tayal. All rights reserved.

Library of Congress Cataloging-in-Publication Data
Names: Hering, Marianne, author. | Hohn, David, date illustrator.
Title: Trouble on the orphan train / Marianne Hering ; cover illustrated by David Hohn ; interior illustrated by Rembrandt and David Hohn.
Description: Carol Stream, Illinois : Tyndale House Publishers, Inc., 2016 | Series: Imagination Station ; book 18 | "Focus on the Family." | "Adventures in Odyssey." | Summary: While searching for Eugene, who is missing somewhere in time, time-travelling cousins Patick and Beth arrive on an orphan train heading west in 1874 and befriend an orphan falsely accused of being part of a train robbery.
Identifiers: LCCN 2016016006 | ISBN 9781589978058 (alk. paper)
Subjects: | CYAC: Time travel—Fiction. | Orphan trains—Fiction. | Orphans—Fiction. | Cousins—Fiction. | Christian life—Fiction.
Classification: LCC PZ7.H431258 Tq 2016 | DDC [Fic]—dc23 LC record available at https://lccn.loc.gov/2016016006

Printed in the United States of America

23 22 21 20 19 18 17
8   7   6   5   4   3   2

For manufacturing information regarding this product, please call 1-800-323-9400.

For information about special discounts for bulk purchases, please contact Tyndale House Publishers at csresponse@tyndale.com or call 800-323-9400.

Contents

Prologue

At Whit's End, a lightning storm zapped the Imagination Station's computer. Then the Imagination Station began to do strange things. It took Patrick to the wrong adventure. The machine was also giving the wrong gifts.

At the workshop, Mr. Whittaker was gone. Eugene was in charge.

Beth uncovered an older version of the Imagination Station. It looked like a car. But this machine had some unusual features. It had lockdown mode. Lockdown mode took passengers to a new place. But the

passengers couldn't get out of the Imagination Station. They could only watch what was happening. At the end of book 17, *In Fear of the Spear*, Eugene was missing somewhere in history. Beth and Patrick were trying to find him. They didn't know which Imagination Station to ride in.

Here's what happened:

● ● ●

Patrick couldn't decide which one to pick.

"Let's go in the helicopter one," Beth said.

"No," Patrick said. "It's still damaged from the lightning strike."

"Well," Beth said, "why not the car one?"

"That one's worse. Eugene got in it with me, but he disappeared," Patrick said.

"The Imagination Station sent you on different adventures!" Beth said. "It's never happened before."

"I don't know where or when Eugene went," Patrick said.

Beth said, "Think, Patrick. What happened?"

Patrick closed his eyes to help him remember. "Right before Eugene disappeared, he said something weird," Patrick said.

"Tell me," Beth said.

Patrick looked worried. "I heard Eugene say, 'Stop the train!' He sounded scared."

"So these are the choices," Beth said. She held up her index finger. "Option one, get into a broken machine."

Patrick looked at the helicopter Imagination Station. It had taken him to Pompeii by mistake. And it had taken Beth here instead of back to Whit's End.

Beth held up a second finger. "Option two, get into an Imagination Station that lands on a moving train."

"Or worse, on the train track," Patrick said.

Patrick looked at the car machine. It had been working fine until this last adventure. But Mr. Whittaker had programmed it for the government to use. Maybe it had hidden features that were causing problems.

"Maybe we should just stay here," Patrick said. "Mr. Whittaker will come find us."

"When?" Beth asked. "No one knows the day he's coming back."

Patrick sighed. "Let's take the car one," he said. "It has a lockdown mode. If it's too dangerous, it won't let us out."

"And maybe it will take us to Eugene," she said.

Patrick shrugged. "If it doesn't separate us too," he said.

The cousins sat in the comfortable black seats. They shut the doors.

Patrick gave the steering wheel a big spin.

Colors flashed on the windshield. They whirled like a kaleidoscope.

Patrick heard the shriek of a train whistle.

And suddenly everything went black.

The Train Station

Patrick watched the Imagination Station vanish. He quickly looked around at his new surroundings.

He was standing on a wood platform. He saw a nearby sign on a wood post. It was shaped like an X and said RAILROAD CROSSING.

Then he remembered he wasn't alone. At least he shouldn't be.

He turned around and saw a small

gray wood building. It had a door and two windows. A wood sign was on the side of the building. It said Hogan Mountain.

But there was no Beth. He shouted her name twice. No one answered. He shouted for Eugene. But again, no one answered.

A mountain stood in the distance. Train tracks and dirt roads crisscrossed the area. Patrick saw nothing else except countryside. Pines, oaks, and rocky hillsides spread out before him.

Patrick looked down. His shoes were black boots. They laced up to his ankles. He had on black knee-high socks and black knickers.

He groaned. "I don't like knickers," he whispered to himself. "They're too short for pants and too long for shorts."

He stretched out his arms. He was

wearing a jacket that matched the knickers. He was glad for the jacket. The air had a chill to it.

He felt his neck. A bow tie. "And bow ties look goofy," he said louder.

Patrick moved toward the building. The building was obviously empty. There were posters nailed to the wall near the door. Most of the posters said WANTED at the top. All of them showed faces of scowling men.

One fellow had a straight nose with a thick moustache. The governor of Missouri would pay a ten-thousand-dollar reward for him, dead or alive. The outlaw's name was Jesse James.

An off-white envelope caught Patrick's eye. It had the words "To

Patrick." The words were handwritten in black ink. He pulled the envelope off the wall. It was sealed.

Just then Patrick heard the faint whistle of a train.

Patrick couldn't wait to open the envelope. He started to tear it. But the train whistle blew again. This time it shrieked much louder.

He would have to wait to read the letter.

Patrick rushed to the platform. The train was approaching the station. Smoke gushed from the engine's smokestack.

The engine car rolled past Patrick slowly. It had a large number seven on the front.

The engineer stuck his head and an arm out the window. He wore a gray cloth cap. He waved at Patrick.

Patrick waved back.

Then the fuel car slowly rolled past. It was loaded with wood.

A long railcar was next. It said Adams Express Company on the side. The express-car door was open.

The train came to a full stop.

The passenger cars had lots of windows. Patrick saw faces looking out at him. Most people were smiling. *Could Beth or Eugene be on that train?* he wondered.

One boy in the last car stared at Patrick. The boy stuck out his tongue. Then he kept staring.

Patrick scowled. He thought the boy was rude.

A door on the passenger car opened. A tall, bearded man stepped off the train.

11

He checked his pocket watch. His watch was gold too.

The man's blue uniform had gold buttons. He wore a matching blue cap.

"Hello," the man said to Patrick. "I'm Conductor Alford. May I punch your ticket?"

Patrick's heart sank. *Ticket?*

Patrick felt in the pockets of his knickers. There was something in his right pocket. He pulled it out. He found three pieces of hard candy, but no ticket.

Patrick felt in his jacket pockets. Nothing was there except the letter. He gulped. "I didn't know I needed a ticket," he mumbled.

The conductor frowned. He said, "Young man, you can't ride the train alone. Where are your parents?"

The Newsboy

The Imagination Station stilled. Beth looked out the windshield. She could see a busy city street.

The buildings were tall and made of brick. There were lampposts in front of the buildings. The people wore old-fashioned clothes and hats. Horses pulled wagons, carts, or buggies.

Beth turned toward Patrick to say something. But his seat was empty!

"Not again," she muttered.

Beth pulled on the door handle. It wouldn't budge.

"Let me out!" she shouted at the machine. She pounded on the glass. She leaned her shoulder against the door and pushed.

Nothing happened. Beth was trapped inside.

This must be lockdown mode, she thought. *But where's the danger?*

The Imagination Station began to roll forward as if in response. It moved along the street.

Beth thought the machine was following a young boy. His clothes were barely more than rags. His face and hands were black with dirt. He had a stack of newspapers underneath his arm.

The boy was shouting, "Get the *Tribune*! Two cents!"

The newsboy caught up with some men in brown suits. One of the men bought a paper. He handed money to the newsboy. The boy dropped the pennies into the pocket of his knickers.

Just then, Beth heard a voice. It was coming from three speakers in the machine's ceiling.

The Imagination Station's speakers blared. "In the 1870s, New York City was filled with crime. The jails held more than eight hundred children ages nine and up. Thirty thousand more children lived on the streets."

Beth heard a strange noise. It was like a birdcall or a whistle. *Why-o! Why-o!* She couldn't tell what had made the sound.

The voice in the Imagination Station said, "One street gang of youths was known as

the Whyos. They were named after their
bird-like gang signal. For twenty-five dollars,
a member would shoot someone in the leg."

That's awful, Beth thought.

She focused on the newsboy. He hollered,
"Jesse James robs stagecoach! Read all
about it!"

Beth saw an older boy in a green cap.
He seemed to be watching the newsboy.
The older boy cupped his hands over his
mouth. He blew into his hands and made
a noise . . . *Why-o*.

He must be in the Whyos gang, Beth
thought.

The boy in the green cap ran over to
the newsboy. He grabbed the smaller boy
by the arm. He dragged him into an alley.
Copies of the *Tribune* scattered everywhere.

The Imagination Station rolled into the

alley. Beth could see that there was no back entrance. The newsboy was trapped.

"You're selling newspapers on the Whyos's street," the bigger boy said. "Hand over your money or else!"

Beth wanted to help the newsboy. She shouted, "Police! Police!" But no one could hear her.

She punched the car's horn. It didn't work. All she could do was watch the robbery.

The newsboy said, "The money is in my boot." He bent down. Suddenly he threw some sand in the gang member's face.

The older boy took a step back. He rubbed his eyes.

The newsboy tried to get out of the alley. But the other boy blocked him.

"I won't let you rob me," the newsboy said.

Beth could see his two front teeth were missing.

"We'll see about that," the older boy said. Then he used his hands to whistle *Why-o, why-o.*

Three more youths came running into the alley. They surrounded the newsboy.

The Imagination Station's windshield started to spin with colors. Beth couldn't see what was going on.

"Go back to New York," she shouted at the machine. "I need to know what happens!"

● ● ●

Patrick gave Mr. Alford a weak smile. Then he looked at the boards of the platform. "My parents aren't here," Patrick said truthfully.

The conductor took off his cap. He knelt next to Patrick. "Tell me, have you seen your parents recently?" Mr. Alford asked kindly.

Patrick didn't know how to answer. Time was different in the Imagination Station. Finally he asked, "What day is it exactly?"

The conductor chuckled. "Today is
Saturday, January 31, 1874, in the year
of our Lord," he said.

"Wow, 1874," Patrick said. He scratched
his head. "It's been centuries since I've seen
my parents."

A look of pity crossed Mr. Alford's
face. "You've been alone a long time," he
said. The conductor stood up and patted
Patrick's head. "I think I know someone
who can help."

Mr. Alford put a hand on Patrick's
arm. Then he guided Patrick toward the
passenger car.

Patrick sighed with relief. All he wanted
was to read the letter and find Eugene. No
one was here, so that meant getting on this
train.

Patrick followed Mr. Alford to the passenger

car. The door in the center of the car was open. Patrick stepped up the three stairs and onto the railcar. He stood just inside.

A little heating stove was near the door. Pretty lamps hung from the ceiling. The seats were covered in gold-and-red fabric.

A few adults sat in pairs up front. Five children were clustered at the back of the car. There were two girls and three boys.

Suddenly something firm and moist hit Patrick's forehead. Then it bounced off.

Patrick rubbed his forehead. He looked at the ground. A small, bruised apple lay on the red carpet.

Mr. Alford hadn't

noticed the flying fruit. He had moved
toward the back of the car. He was talking
to a woman passenger.

Patrick picked up the small apple. He
scanned the passengers' faces.
No one seemed to be looking
at him.

Then Patrick's eyes locked
with a boy's. It was the
same kid who had stuck
out his tongue. The boy
grinned at him.

Children's Aid Society

The Imagination Station window cleared.
The scene from the alley was gone. Beth
could now see a group of children in fine
clothes. They stood on the steps of a white
country church.

The children looked clean and happy.
Each had a small cardboard suitcase.

A man and a woman were watching
the children. The adults were dressed in
formal, black clothes. The man opened the

church door. The children walked quietly inside.

The woman wore a large black hat covered in a bouquet of white flowers. She followed the last of the children into the church.

The Imagination Station's speakers blared. "The Children's Aid Society found homes for New York City's orphans. The children were placed on trains and sent to the country. Social workers, called agents, cared for the children until they were adopted.

The voice continued. "Many children found homes and were raised as sons or daughters. Older orphans found jobs and were provided with food and lodging. All of the orphans got to attend school."

"That's so cool," Beth said.

The Imagination Station followed the children. The machine bumped up the stairs. It was too wide to fit through the church door. Then, mysteriously, the machine appeared inside the church.

Beth gasped. She had never traveled through a wall before.

The children stood on a raised area near the pulpit. They were lined up in a row. A group of townsfolk was in the audience. The men and women sat in the pews.

Each orphan stepped forward one at a time. The boy or girl told everyone his or her name.

A red-haired girl said her name was Gracie. She gave a little curtsy.

One boy looked familiar to Beth. He stepped forward and smiled.

Beth knew him at once. She saw the missing front teeth. It was the newsboy from the city. His name was Leonard Wilcox.

Leonard bowed. Then he raised his hands. He stuck his thumbs in each ear and waggled his fingers. Then he bowed again.

Beth giggled. But the woman agent in black didn't. She walked over to Leonard and whispered in his ear. She took him by the arm and led him off the stage.

Beth realized that the kids were showing off. They wanted to be adopted. Leonard had appeared rude. No wonder the agent took him off the stage.

Next, Gracie and two little boys sang a hymn. Beth knew the tune from church.

It was "Fairest Lord Jesus." The audience clapped loudly afterward.

Then one tall, strong-looking boy recited a long Bible passage. It had something to do with sheep and green grass. An older man and a gray-haired woman in the pews stood up. Beth guessed that they were married.

"We'll take him," the man said. "We need someone to help with the farm. We need an honest, God-fearing boy to be our son. We lost our own two boys in the war."

The boy's face had a strange expression. His eyes gleamed, but his mouth fell open. He looked happy and scared all at once.

Beth wondered what he was thinking. He'd never even talked to those people. Yet they would be his new parents!

Suddenly the Imagination Station's

windshield was covered in bright colors. The colors began to whirl. Beth couldn't see what was happening anymore.

She yanked the machine's door handle. The door flew open.

All at once, Beth found herself falling.

Patrick stared at the boy who threw the apple. He was wearing a jacket, knickers, and a bow tie just like Patrick's. He was missing his front teeth. He slid his tongue through the gap and wriggled it.

Just then Mr. Alford said, "Patrick, I'd like you to meet Miss Cookson. She's an agent for the Children's Aid Society."

Patrick quickly shoved the apple into his pocket.

Miss Cookson rose from her seat. She

walked up the aisle toward him. Mr. Alford followed her.

Miss Cookson was wearing a long black skirt and cape. She held a small black-satin purse. Several large fake lilies were on her floppy hat.

Patrick thought she looked all set to attend a funeral. She was wearing the right color. And she could just leave the flowered hat on

the grave. It would make a nice bouquet.

"Miss Cookson," the conductor said, "this boy is in need. Perhaps the Children's Aid Society can help him."

Miss Cookson smiled at Patrick. Her face seemed nice. It was round with rosy cheeks.

"God's grace is with you," Miss Cookson said. "Several of our orphans have found homes already."

"What's that got to do with me?" Patrick asked.

Miss Cookson opened her purse. She took out a thick piece of paper. It was the size of an index card.

"Those children aren't riding the last part of the orphan line," she said. "I have extra tickets."

She handed the conductor the piece of paper.

Mr. Alford pulled a metal hole puncher out of his pants pocket. He punched a star-shaped hole through the ticket. He handed it to Patrick.

"Don't lose this," Mr. Alford said. "I need to punch your ticket at every stop."

"Thank you!" Patrick said.

Mr. Alford left the car.

Patrick put the ticket in his jacket pocket next to Eugene's letter.

He scanned the passenger car. He didn't see Eugene or Beth. There were several empty seats. He planned to sit down and read the letter.

He chose an empty seat in the front of the car. But Miss Cookson motioned for him to stand up.

"All the orphans must sit in the back," she said. "Come this way, please."

Miss Cookson led Patrick to the orphans. The two girls and two younger boys were sitting in one row. Patrick spotted the boy who had thrown the apple. He was surrounded by three empty seats.

Figures, Patrick thought. *No one wants to sit near that kid.*

Miss Cookson introduced the boys to each other. "Patrick," she said, "please take the window seat next to Leonard. You'll become good friends."

Patrick doubted that. But he was willing to try.

Leonard smiled. He seemed happy to meet Patrick.

Then Miss Cookson turned around to return to her seat.

Patrick tried to pass Leonard to get to the window seat. But Leonard blocked his way. Then he stuck out his tongue.

"I need to sit down," Patrick said, scowling. "Let me pass."

"Do you like apples?" Leonard whispered. "I do. I wish I had mine back."

Patrick didn't want to return the apple. He had a feeling that Leonard would throw the apple again. But the apple didn't belong to him.

So Patrick took the apple out of his pocket. He held it out to Leonard as a gesture of friendship.

Leonard ignored the apple. He stood up.

"Miss Cookson!" Leonard shouted. "The new boy just took my apple!"

● ● ●

Beth's head felt dizzy. All around her were spinning colors. The air was cold. Her lungs hurt when she breathed.

She had no idea how long she fell. Or if she was really falling at all.

Moments later Beth found herself tumbling on some grass. She rolled down a short hill. Her elbow banged into a rock.

"Ouch!" she said. She stood up and rubbed her bare arm. She looked around for the Imagination Station. It wasn't there. It may have never even landed.

Beth was on a little hill overlooking a small wood building. It was painted gray. Pines, oaks, elms, and other trees surrounded the area. Vines were growing everywhere.

Beth could also see a railroad-crossing sign and train tracks. A small train was stopped in front of the building. But she couldn't see who was getting on or off. The building blocked her view.

The air smelled fresh and smoky at the same time. A chilly breeze whipped through the trees. She shivered and wished she had a coat.

Beth looked at her clothes. She was in a nice white cotton dress. Her shoes were sturdy black boots with black shoelaces.

She reached for the dress collar. The fabric had a pattern. It felt like lace.

Just then she saw something small falling from the sky. It was coming straight toward her.

Beth stepped aside and covered her head. A yellow gourd landed near her feet. The gourd bounced and rolled a bit before stopping.

Beth picked it up. It was dry and hollow. Inside she found a small book, a large tooth, and a bottle of medicine.

The book title was *English-Waodani Dictionary*. The medicine was to stop infections. The tooth looked as if it was from a jaguar.

"The wrong gifts again," she said to herself. "The Imagination Station is still acting wonky."

She put the tooth in her dress pocket. But she left the gourd on the grass. She walked toward the train tracks and building.

Suddenly a whistle blew three times.

The train was leaving! Had Patrick or Eugene gotten on the train?

Beth ran as fast as she could down the hill.

The Apple

Miss Cookson turned around when Leonard shouted. She didn't look kind anymore. She was frowning sternly. Her eyes were black and beady like an eagle's.

Patrick gulped. He did appear to have stolen the apple. It was in his hand.

Leonard started to cry. "Send the new boy away, Miss Cookson!" he said. "He's a thief."

Patrick was amazed that the boy could act so well. Leonard truly sounded frightened. And his tears were real. Droplets rolled down his cheeks.

"I know this looks bad, ma'am," Patrick said. "But—"

"There will be no tale telling," Miss Cookson said. "Return the apple at once."

Patrick wanted to roll his eyes in exasperation. But he blinked several times instead. Inside he was counting to ten. *One, two, three . . .*

Slowly he handed the apple to Leonard.

The orphan boy's tears were still flowing. He sniffled a few times. Then he reached for the apple.

"Ew," Leonard said. "It's mushed." He looked at Patrick. "You bruised it."

Four, five, six . . . Patrick counted higher.

Leonard lifted the apple to show Miss Cookson. It did have a large brown spot on one side.

"Whoever bruised that apple was wasteful," Miss Cookson said. "I'm speechless."

So was Patrick. "I, I, I . . ." was all he could say.

Leonard leaned a little toward Patrick. He whispered so only Patrick could hear. "If I had some candy," he said, "I might sit down and be quiet."

Patrick's anger was boiling. *Seven, eight, nine* . . . He choked back angry words.

Patrick shoved his hand into the right pocket of his knickers. He pulled out a piece of candy. "Here," he muttered. He opened his hand and showed Leonard the wrapped sweet.

"I saw from the window. I know you have *three* pieces," Leonard whispered.

Patrick ground his teeth together. He took out the other pieces of candy. He held out all three. *Ten!*

Leonard snatched the candy from Patrick's palm. Instantly his tears stopped. He sat down and unwrapped one piece. He popped it into his mouth.

The train whistled three long bursts of sound. Then the bell rang. The locomotive began to move.

Miss Cookson seemed satisfied that Leonard was happy. She moved down the aisle two rows and sat down.

Patrick was not going to sit next to Leonard. This time he chose a pair of seats across the aisle. He sat in the window seat and turned his back to Leonard. He took out the letter from his jacket pocket.

He needed more light to read. He lifted the window shade. Patrick peered outside.

The train was pulling away from the platform.

And Beth was running alongside the locomotive. She was yelling at the engineer.

"Stop the train!" she shouted. She waved her arms. "Stop the train!"

5

Beth

Beth kept her eye on the train. Streams of smoke puffed out of the smokestack.

The great black wheels groaned as they turned. The long rods moved slowly up and down as the wheels rolled.

Loud hissing sounds came from the engine. A cloud of steam spewed from underneath the train.

The heat washed over Beth. She ran in a wider arc to avoid being burned.

"Stop the train!" she shouted again.

⬤ ⬤ ⬤

Patrick needed to get to the back door. It was behind Patrick's and Leonard's row of seats. Patrick sneaked to the door.

Leonard was watching. But Patrick didn't care. "No tale telling," he said to Leonard.

Patrick grabbed the doorknob, turned, and pulled. The door swung open. He quietly sneaked out. He closed the door softly.

Patrick stepped outside onto a wide platform. A gust of wind washed over him. He swayed a bit and grabbed the railing to steady himself.

The train began to really roll now. The

squeaks and groans of the wheels and rods were loud.

Just then he saw Beth running alongside the train. She looked out of breath. Her face was red with effort. Her arms were pumping wildly.

Patrick shouted, "Don't give up!"

Beth was falling farther back. Soon the train would pass her.

Patrick heard the *clickety-clack* noises of the tracks. He heard the metal wheels grinding as they turned.

Patrick also heard someone behind him. He looked over his shoulder. Leonard was there, right behind him. The boy grinned.

"I'm not tale telling," Leonard said.

Beth was running full speed right beside the last car. Her dress was flapping in the wind. Her hair was bouncing on her back with each stride.

Patrick scuttled down the platform stairs. He leaned over. He bent as low to the ground as he could get. He stretched out his arm and called to Beth, "Grab my hand!"

"She'll never make it!" Leonard shouted. "She can't run fast enough!"

Patrick felt Leonard's hands on his back.

He's going to push me off the train, Patrick thought.

Patrick looked over his shoulder. "Leave me alone!" he shouted at the orphan.

Just then Patrick felt Beth's hand grab his wrist. He swung his head around and focused his attention on her. He clasped her wrist and pulled.

Beth lifted off the ground, but not high
enough. She landed on the ground again.
She was still running.

Patrick felt her hand slipping from his
wrist. He grabbed her palm this time.
He squeezed her knuckles as hard as
he could.

Just then, Leonard's arms wrapped
around Patrick's waist. The boy
pulled Patrick backward and
anchored him.

Patrick gave a mighty
tug. Suddenly Beth was

on the stairs. She fell on top of him. Patrick leaned back into Leonard.

"Ow!" Leonard said. "Don't squish me."

The three children crawled and shuffled away from danger. They scrambled farther back to the safety of the platform.

Beth was gasping for breath. "Thank you," she said, panting.

Patrick's heart was pounding. He couldn't believe Beth was safe. And he couldn't believe that Leonard had helped.

"Thank you, Leonard," Patrick said. "Beth would be walking if it wasn't for you."

Leonard shrugged. "I just want to see you get in trouble," he said. "Miss Cookson's gonna give you a tongue-lashing."

6

The Letter

Beth's breathing steadied as she sat on the platform. She flexed the hand that Patrick had squeezed. The pain was going away.

A gentle breeze blew in her face. The train was chugging along now. The platform vibrated with motion. The car swayed slightly whenever the train tracks curved.

A woman stepped out onto the platform. She wore black clothes and a large black hat with white flowers.

"Leonard! Patrick!" the woman said sternly. Her hands were on her hips. "I have looked all over the train. You boys have some explaining—"

Miss Cookson stopped taking when she saw Beth sitting next to Patrick.

"Hello," Beth said with a smile. She recognized this woman as the agent from the Children's Aid Society.

Beth stood up. "My name is Beth," she said. "I'm Patrick's cousin. I got on at the back of the train because I was late." She held out her hand for a handshake.

Miss Cookson looked stunned. She gently squeezed the tips of Beth's fingers with her own.

"Where are your parents?" Miss Cookson asked.

Beth gulped. She didn't know how to answer truthfully. She looked to Patrick for a clue.

But Patrick's face was hidden in his hands. He was no help.

"My parents," Beth said slowly, "are with Patrick's parents."

Miss Cookson gave Beth's hand another gentle squeeze. Then she let it go.

"I'm so sorry your parents aren't with us," Miss Cookson said. "But the Children's Aid Society can help you."

Beth nodded.

"It's very strange that you weren't on

the station platform with Patrick," Miss Cookson said. "What made you dillydally?"

Beth blushed. "I heard the whistle and bell only at the last minute," she said softly. "I was behind the train station. My imagination kind of ran away with me. It seemed as if I had been in another world."

Apparently Miss Cookson was not fond of creativity. "Let's talk no more about such fanciful subjects," she said. "Orphans need a good dose of reality."

Miss Cookson then sent Leonard back inside. Leonard obeyed.

Then Miss Cookson looked down at Patrick.

He stood up and straightened his suit jacket. "Ma'am?" he said.

"Why didn't you tell me you had a cousin?" Miss Cookson asked.

"I hoped she was already on board," Patrick said. "I didn't see her inside the station. And she wasn't on the platform."

Miss Cookson sighed and shook her head. She seemed annoyed. Then she motioned the cousins to get inside the railcar.

"I'll get Beth a ticket once you're seated," Miss Cookson said. "Conductor Alford is not going to like this at all."

Beth went in first and then Patrick. Miss Cookson was last.

Miss Cookson assigned Beth a seat in the passenger car. She let Beth and Patrick sit together. Leonard was across the aisle. He had an empty seat next to him.

"I'm going to find Mr. Alford about Beth's ticket," she said to all three of them. "Stay seated and be polite."

"Yes, ma'am," Patrick said.

"Thank you, Miss Cookson," Beth said.

Leonard only grinned.

Miss Cookson left the passenger car. Leonard leaned across the aisle. He grinned at Beth. He pulled an envelope out from the inside pocket of his jacket.

"What will you give me if I give you this?" Leonard said. He waved the envelope at Patrick.

Patrick wanted to snatch the envelope out of Leonard's hand. He reached across Beth and tried to grab it.

But Leonard was faster. The orphan put the envelope back in his jacket. "Be careful," he said, "or the letter might get burned." He nodded his head toward the woodstove four rows up.

Patrick got angry and pointed a finger at the orphan. "You pickpocket!" he said to Leonard. "You weren't trying to help me get Beth on board. You were stealing from my jacket pocket!"

Leonard grinned. "I wanted more candy," he said.

"I'll tell Miss Cookson," Patrick said. "I can prove the letter is mine."

"Miss Cookson doesn't listen to tale telling," Leonard said with a smirk.

Beth pulled the jaguar tooth out of her dress pocket. She held it up by her first finger and thumb.

Patrick recognized the

shape of the tooth. It was like some he'd seen before in the rain forest. That meant the gifts were getting mixed up.

Beth moved the tooth back and forth. Leonard's brown eyes followed the movement of the tooth. He slowly reached out a hand toward it.

Patrick leaned across Beth and pushed Leonard's arm down. "Use your eyes," Patrick said, "not your hands."

Beth smiled. She closed her fist over the tooth. "Anyway," she said, "the jaguar tooth is mine."

Leonard's eyes bulged. "A *real* jaguar tooth?" he asked.

"Of course," Beth said. "It's worth way more than a letter."

Patrick knew the orphan had outsmarted him again. He sighed.

"Beth," Patrick said, "the letter is from Eugene. Give him the tooth."

Beth shook her head. "Nothing Eugene has to say is worth that much," she said.

Patrick was now getting angry at Beth, too. He said, "That letter is important, and you know it." His tone of voice was tense.

Beth glared at him. "The tooth is too valuable," she said calmly. "And that's a fact." She looked at Leonard. "What else do you have?"

Leonard jammed his hands into his knickers pockets. He pulled out two pieces of candy and a penny. He put them in Beth's hand.

Beth looked at the candy and the penny. She shook

her head. "That's not enough," she said. "But you can do something for me."

"What?" Leonard asked.

Beth smirked. "Promise that you'll stop stealing," she said.

"It's a deal!" Leonard said, grinning.

Beth held out her hand. "The letter first," she said.

Leonard reached inside his jacket. He handed her the envelope.

Beth leaned across the aisle. She put the tooth in Leonard's hand.

"Be good now," Beth said. "No more stealing, okay? You're not a Whyos gang member."

Leonard frowned. "How did you know about them?" he asked.

Beth smirked again. "I know lots of things," she said.

Leonard put his hands in his pockets.

"Okay," he said. "I promise, no stealing."

"He's got his fingers crossed," Patrick said. "You can't trust him."

Beth whispered, "Never mind him now. Just open the envelope."

Patrick slid his finger underneath the envelope flap. He neatly tore the paper. Inside were two train tickets and a folded piece of paper.

Patrick took out the letter and unfolded it. He showed it to Beth.

Dear Patrick (and Beth if you're together now),

If you have this letter, it means you landed at the Hogan Mountain, Missouri, train station. I waited there for about two days. No one familiar appeared, and so I headed south. I plan to assist the Pinkerton agents to gather evidence about a recent stagecoach robbery. Jesse James and his gang are believed to have committed the crime. It is to this end I believe Mr. Whittaker programmed this adventure. Come immediately to Little Rock on the number 7 train.

> Your friend,
> Eugene

PS: Don't travel on January 31. It would be disastrous. That's the day J J and gang robbed a train.

Beth wondered what day it was. She glanced at Patrick. Her answer was in his face.

Patrick's mouth was shaped like an O. His face was as white as milk.

"Today's January 31, isn't it?" Beth said.

The Horseman

"Eugene could be wrong," Patrick said. "He might have mixed up the date."

Beth took the letter out of Patrick's hands. She folded it up. Then she put it back in the envelope. "When was the last time Eugene made a mistake?" she asked.

Patrick thought Beth was right. Eugene's memory could be trusted. He probably hadn't made a mistake since kindergarten.

He took the envelope from Beth. He put it back in his jacket pocket.

"Maybe Eugene and the Pinkerton agents will catch Jesse James," Patrick said. "Then he won't rob this train."

"The letter said 'gather evidence,' not 'capture,' " Beth said. "Eugene can't change major events of history. The Imagination Station won't let him."

"But the Imagination Station isn't working properly," Patrick said. "*Anything* could happen."

Patrick leaned forward and glanced across the aisle at Leonard. He didn't want the boy to overhear them.

Leonard had shifted over to the window seat. His forehead was pressed against the glass. He seemed to be intently watching something.

Patrick noticed movement at the front end of the car. Mr. Alford and Miss Cookson were entering the passenger car. They began to walk down the aisle.

Patrick nudged Beth. "Here comes the conductor and Miss Cookson," he said. "Do we tell them about Jesse James?"

"I don't think they would believe us," Beth said.

Miss Cookson walked primly down the aisle. Her small purse was clutched in her hand. She stood in the aisle next to the cousins.

Mr. Alford followed her. He was so tall that his head nearly

bumped the ceiling lamps. Every few steps he had to duck to miss one.

He came to the back of the train. He scanned the orphan section.

"Which girl is our latecomer?" Mr. Alford asked.

Beth raised her hand. "Here, Mr. Conductor," she said. "I'm sorry I had to jump on board."

Mr. Alford said kindly, "That's all right, miss." He patted Beth on the shoulder. "You're an orphan, after all. You probably didn't know any better."

Miss Cookson handed Beth a train ticket. "Mr. Alford has been very generous," she said. "Please remember that and follow his example."

Phew, Patrick thought. *We missed the tongue-lashing.*

Mr. Alford took Beth's ticket and his hole puncher. He poked a little star in the ticket. He handed it back to Beth.

Beth said thank you.

Mr. Alford took out his gold pocket watch. "Ten minutes till we reach Des Arc, Missouri," he said.

Leonard turned his attention away from the window. "Mr. Alford, there's a fellow on a horse following us," he said. His voice was loud with excitement. "I think you should look."

Mr. Alford leaned over and rested his hand on the seat's back. "By golly," he said. "There *is* a man coming along the tracks. He's working that horse mighty hard."

The people with window seats on Leonard's side looked out the window too.

Beth whispered to Patrick, "Do you think it's Jesse James?"

"I don't know," Patrick said. "Let's get a better look."

Beth noticed the train was slowing down. The Missouri hills were steep on this section of the line. A man on a horse could gain ground on it.

Patrick crossed the aisle. He moved to an empty set of seats.

Beth followed Patrick and looked out the window.

The man was wearing a brown hat and a white shirt. His horse was gray and white.

The engineer blew the train's whistle.

There was one long whistle followed by three short blows.

The man on horseback took off his hat. He waved it in a wide arc.

Mr. Alford turned from the window. He quickly moved away from Leonard's seat.

"What did those whistles mean?" Leonard asked the conductor.

"That whistle pattern means we're coming to a stop," Mr. Alford said. "I've got to see to the first-class guests in the sleeper car."

Mr. Alford headed out the front door.

Beth watched the conductor leave and then said softly, "It's not Jesse James."

"Is too," Patrick said. "Who else would be out there?"

"I don't know. But this horseman isn't trying to hide," Beth said. "He wants to be seen."

She rolled her eyes. "Any robber with a

brain would plan a surprise," Beth said. "He would wear a mask and attack at night."

Leonard's face suddenly appeared at the window next to theirs. "Or ruin up the tracks," the orphan said. "That's what Jesse James did in Iowa."

"What happened then?" she asked.

"The train's engine fell over sideways," Leonard said. "Then someone blew up the safe. Everyone's money was stolen."

Beth gasped.

Patrick said, "You're making it up. Stuff like that happens only on TV."

"On TV?" Leonard asked.

"It's not important," Beth said. "Did you read about him in the *Tribune*?"

Leonard nodded. He pulled a small piece of newsprint out of his knickers pocket. "There," he said. He held it out.

Patrick took the newsprint and skimmed the article.

He said to Beth, "Jesse James and gang robbed a stagecoach. That was two weeks ago. A few months ago he robbed a train in Iowa. And in Kentucky, he robbed a bank."

"What about the Pinkerton detectives?" Beth asked. "Why can't they stop him?"

Leonard said, "Because gangs are smart. No one can catch the Whyos either." He took the paper back. "They call the Jesse James gang 'brazen' and 'bold.'"

The train's whistle blew several long blasts.

Mr. Alford opened the back door. Cold air came in with the conductor.

He hurried up the aisle. "There's a fire at the Des Arc

station," Mr. Alford said. "Everyone stay seated."

No one did. The passengers all rushed to the windows. Leonard moved to the opposite side of the train.

"Another train is on fire," Leonard said. "One of the cargo cars has flames as high as the treetops."

Beth looked out the window at the horseman. He was almost at the station too.

She felt a chill. And it wasn't because of the cold.

The Cotton Fire

Patrick watched the train workers battle the orange flames.

First the men detached the cargo car from the other cars. This gave the men space to work. It also kept the sparks from drifting to the other cars.

Patrick could hear the loud crackling and snapping of the fire. The smoke mingled with the clouds, and the sky turned even darker.

Workers near the station were stomping on flying sparks.

A line of bucket carriers formed. Men brought water from a stream that flowed behind the station. Men perching on the side of the cargo car took the buckets. Then those men hoisted the buckets up to douse the fire.

Several male passengers from the number 7 got out to help. Even a man from the first-class sleeper car joined in.

"I'm going out there too," Patrick said to Beth.

Beth opened her mouth to say something. But Patrick didn't wait to hear it. He left through the back door.

"Keep a lookout for Jesse James," Beth shouted after him.

Patrick approached the fire. The heat

was intense. His face began to sweat as he neared the burning cargo car. No campfire he'd ever been near was this powerful.

Ashes floated through the air. A large, white tuft landed at his feet. Cotton was burning.

He joined the men who were carrying buckets of water. Someone put a bucket in front of him. He picked up the handle with one hand and lifted. The bucket wouldn't move.

Patrick put two hands on the handle and lifted. This time the bucket got four inches off the ground. Then he dropped it.

"Mind if I help?" a man asked. "I'm Reverend Hagerty."

Patrick recognized him as the passenger from the sleeper car. He was in a dark suit with a high white collar. His bow tie was a bit crooked. He had a thick beard like Mr. Alford's.

"I can't lift that much water," Patrick said. "It's too heavy."

"Tell you the truth," the reverend said, "I'm getting tired. I could use a hand. Let's share the load."

Patrick stood on one side of the bucket. The reverend stood on the other. Each put one hand on the bucket handle. Together they lifted the bucket.

"Much better," Reverend Hagerty said. "Now let's move toward the fire."

Patrick could now see the cargo car up close. It was full of burning cotton bales.

The flames were now only a few feet high. The fire hissed when a bucketful of water was dumped on it.

Patrick and Reverend Hagerty made seven trips with the bucket. Finally the fire was ebbing.

"That's it for a while," a man in overalls said. "We can beat the fire down now."

Patrick used the break to look around. He studied the faces of the men. None of them had the long, straight nose and moustache of Jesse James that Patrick had seen at the station.

But he did recognize one person: Leonard. The orphan was seated on the edge of the cargo car. He was covered in soot. The little guy was beating back the last of the flames with a rug.

● ● ●

Beth was watching the fire from her seat inside the passenger car. Miss Cookson was two rows up with the other children. They were wailing and sniffling. Beth guessed the fire scared them. They needed Miss Cookson's comfort.

Beth felt a tap on her shoulder. She turned around. It was the horseman.

He had on a white shirt and a jacket. The man's jacket was a little damp. He held his wide-brimmed hat in his hands.

Beth had seen a hat just like it. But she couldn't remember where.

"Are you the traveler who got on board late at Hogan Mountain?" the man said.

"I got on at the last stop," Beth said. "Is that the Hogan Mountain depot?"

He nodded. His eyes narrowed. "Did you see anyone or anything that was suspicious?" the horseman asked.

Beth felt nervous. "I, um, was in a hurry,"

she said. "I didn't see much of the depot at all. Just the outhouse."

The horseman laid his hat on a seat. Then he sat down next to her. His long legs barely fit in the space between seats. His boots smelled a little bit like corn chips.

He twisted the ends of his thick moustache.

"I'm Robert Pinkerton," he said. "I'm looking for some missing evidence. It's from a recent stagecoach robbery."

Beth said, "I'm sure I haven't seen it."

"I'll describe it," Mr. Pinkerton said. "You might remember."

"Okay," Beth said, "but—"

Mr. Pinkerton cut in. "It's a saddlebag," he said. "With horseshoes burned into the leather. Inside was a badge—"

It was Beth's turn to interrupt. "It was

star-shaped," she said. "And there were some bandanas, rope, and glasses!"

She clapped her hands. "I remember it now, even the carrots. And a hat went missing too, didn't it? One just like yours!"

Mr. Pinkerton sat forward. "That's right!" He seemed excited now too. "Where did you see it? I need to find it."

Beth froze. Her eyes grew large with fear. She figured out her mistake too late. She couldn't tell Mr. Pinkerton his evidence was in ancient Pompeii.

"I-I-I think," Beth said, "you need to look out for Jesse James. The evidence isn't really important. Here's what is: the James gang is going to rob this train today."

Mr. Pinkerton's eyebrows shifted in

concern. "And how do you know this?" he asked.

"My friend Eugene told me," Beth said.

"Eugene *again*!" Mr. Pinkerton said. "I can't believe it!" He got out of his seat and put on his hat. He leaned over Beth.

Beth shrank in her seat. She hoped Patrick would come back soon. She needed help.

"Stand up, miss," Mr. Pinkerton said. His voice was steely. "You're coming with me."

"But the conductor told me to stay here," Beth said.

"That doesn't matter," Mr. Pinkerton said. "Because you're under arrest!"

The Express Car

The cotton fire at Des Arc was out. The reverend invited Patrick and Leonard to come to the sleeper car.

"You've helped a great deal," Reverend Hagerty said. "You deserve a treat. I'll make sure you boys get some tasty first-class food."

Patrick felt a little guilty going without Beth. But he was tired from all that work.

"Yes, sir!" Leonard said. "Thank you."

Reverend Hagerty left for a moment. He said he was going to tell Miss Cookson where the boys were.

Two women and a few men were traveling in the sleeper car. There were plenty of empty seats and beds. Leonard picked a seat at the back of the car. It was several rows behind the stove.

Patrick climbed into a cushy bed not

too far from Leonard. It was across the aisle from Reverend Hagerty's seat.

The train whistle blew. The engine and the four cars began to move along the tracks again.

Patrick was tired even though it was still daytime. He pulled down the window shade to block the sun. He snuggled into his bunk.

Reverend Hagerty came back and settled in his seat. He began to read a book.

The sleeper car was warm from the stove's heat. The rocking of the train lulled Patrick to sleep in seconds.

Patrick woke for a moment when Mr. Alford came in. The conductor punched his ticket. Mr. Alford said something about Beth. He left a plate of tiny sandwiches near Patrick's pillow.

But Patrick was too tired to pay attention. He fell into a deep sleep.

● ● ●

Mr. Pinkerton took Beth to the Adams Express railcar. They stepped up to the only door. It was on the side of the car.

Beth noticed the car was divided into compartments.

The detective and Beth hurried through the first compartment that held sacks of mail. They went through a second compartment. Baggage was stowed inside that one. The third compartment belonged to the Adams Express Company.

Beth and Mr. Pinkerton went inside. Mr. Pinkerton closed the interior door. There were no windows, only vents near the ceiling.

Another agent was inside the compartment. He wore an all-white suit.

Mr. Pinkerton said, "I'm leaving this girl in your car, Agent Wilson."

Agent Wilson looked confused. "That's unusual," he said.

"She knows too much about Jesse James,"

Mr. Pinkerton said. "She might be a spy for the James gang."

"So that's how he does it!" Agent Wilson said. "I never would have thought to use children."

The train whistle blew. Mr. Pinkerton opened the narrow compartment door.

"Please stay here," Beth said. "Jesse James will come. I know it."

The detective looked at Beth, then tipped his hat. "Miss, I believe you are lying to help the James gang," Mr. Pinkerton said. "He'll be robbing some other train or stagecoach today. The last place Jesse James will be is anywhere near this train."

Mr. Pinkerton closed the interior door behind him. Beth heard his heavy boots trudge through the other compartments.

Then she heard the side door of the railcar slide shut.

Beth guessed Mr. Pinkerton was going to get back on his horse. He was going to ride far away. He wouldn't be there to protect them.

She felt as if it were all her fault.

The train began to chug slowly away from Des Arc.

Agent Wilson sat in the only chair. He looked neat and tidy. Even his vest and tie were white.

Beth looked around for someplace to sit. There was a small table with some packages on it. The stove was too hot to use as a seat.

A black safe was against the wall. It had gold lettering painted on it.

Beth decided to sit on top of it. The safe was so tall that her feet dangled in the air. "What's going to happen to me?" Beth asked.

Agent Wilson said, "I'll keep you here till we get to Little Rock, Arkansas. They have a jail."

Jail? Beth didn't like the sound of that.

"Then what?" Beth asked.

Agent Wilson scratched his head. "I really don't know for sure," he said. "You're the first child criminal I've ever met."

The agent studied her. "You don't look dangerous," he said. "Perhaps it's the lace around your collar. You look like an angel."

Beth smiled her most angelic smile. "I didn't do anything wrong," she said. "I promise. Please let me go back to the passenger car."

"Mr. Pinkerton is a famous detective. He says you may be part of the James gang,"

Agent Wilson said. He shook his head as if
he didn't believe it.

"It's rotten of those brazen bandits to
use children as spies," the agent went on.
"Robbing should be a man's business."

Beth thought that no one should be in the
robbing business.

"Let's hope the train doesn't have
trouble," Agent Wilson said. "Things will go
easier for you at the trial."

Trial? Beth didn't want to go to trial.

She'd have to take an oath and put her
hand on the Bible. Then she'd have to tell
about the Imagination Station. She would
have to mention Patrick. That meant he
might get in trouble too.

Agent Wilson took out a silver pocket
watch. He read the time. "Looks like we
may gain back some of the time we lost.

If so, we should arrive in Little Rock before midnight."

"And if Jesse James attacks this train?" Beth asked. "Who will help us? Mr. Pinkerton just left."

Agent Wilson showed Beth his pistol. It had a fat, black barrel.

"Then it will be the James gang's last robbery," Agent Wilson said. "I intend to capture that scoundrel. No one has stolen anything from me and my pistol yet."

Pistol? Beth hoped the Imagination Station would appear. She wanted nothing to do with guns.

"Then I'll get the ten-thousand-dollar reward," Agent Wilson said. He tucked the pistol back inside his suit jacket. "I'll be rich."

Gad's Hill, Missouri

Patrick's eyes opened slowly. He heard men talking. Leonard was shaking his shoulder. The orphan wasn't being very gentle.

"Leave me alone," Patrick said. He slapped Leonard's hand away.

"If that's what you want," Leonard said. "But you're missing all the fun."

"What?" Patrick said.

"Jesse James and his gang are robbing the train. They will probably start with the

safe. It's in the Adams Express railcar,"
Leonard said. "Then they'll come here."

Patrick got out of the bunk. He looked
around the sleeper car.

The rich men were acting strangely. One
man wore a bowler hat. He was hiding
money in one of his socks. Two others were
ripping up the carpet at the back of the
train.

The two women were crying. They wiped
at their tears with linen handkerchiefs.

Only Reverend Hagerty was calm. He was
sitting still with his hands folded in his lap.
Patrick noticed they were smeared with
soot. One hand looked burned and had a
red and swollen thumb.

Patrick asked the reverend, "Is it true?
Are we being robbed?"

"Something went wrong at the Gad's Hill

stop," Reverend Hagerty said. "A man was waving a red warning flag. So Mr. Alford went to investigate. Now there are horsemen circling the train."

"Why didn't you wake me?" Patrick asked.

"Sleep is a gift from the Lord," the reverend said. "I didn't want to rob you of it. You may soon be robbed of everything else."

Patrick turned and reached toward the cloth window shade.

"Don't touch that," Leonard said.

Patrick lifted up the fabric just an inch anyway.

He peeked outside. A horseman with a rifle was outside. The man was wearing a white hood and a thick, navy-blue coat. He raised his rifle in the air.

"The next person who looks out will regret it," the horseman shouted.

Patrick let go of the window shade and slumped in a seat.

Leonard sat next to him. "Told you so," he said, smirking.

● ● ●

Beth knew something was wrong at the next train stop. So did Agent Wilson. He looked at his silver pocket watch several times.

"We've stopped too long at Gad's Hill," Agent Wilson said. "We should be moving on."

Beth stood on top of the safe. She peeked

out through the slatted vents near the ceiling.

"I can see some men on horses," she said. "But I can't tell what else is out there."

Beth heard the sound of the railcar's door sliding open. It made her heart race.

"Someone's coming," Agent Wilson said in a hushed tone.

Beth quietly got off the safe. She pressed her ear to the compartment wall. "I hear lots of footsteps and thuds," she said. "It sounds like they dropped something."

"That's the luggage and the mailbags," he whispered. "They're looking for cash and jewelry."

Agent Wilson stood. He put his shoulder to the safe. He grunted and leaned against the big iron box. The safe moved slowly away from the wall.

"Get behind that," Agent Wilson said. "The thick metal should stop any bullets."

Should? Beth hoped he was right.

Agent Wilson held his pistol in his right hand. He pressed himself against the wall close to the door.

Beth waited for the men to crash it open. Instead someone knocked three times. She crouched behind the safe and began to pray. She didn't want Agent Wilson to get shot.

Beth heard the click of Agent Wilson's pistol. He was getting ready to fire.

Then a voice said, "Open up, William! These ruffians have a pistol."

Beth gasped. The speaker was Mr. Alford.

Beth heard the door open. She heard boots walking on the wood floors.

"Put down your pistol," a deep voice said. There was the sound of something being put on the table.

"Now open the safe," the voice said. "Or Mr. Alford gets it."

The Diamonds

Leonard elbowed Patrick in the ribs. The boy pointed at one of the women in the sleeper car.

Patrick watched as she got out of her seat. She was wearing a fancy red hat and dress. Her earrings and bracelet sparkled. Extra dress fabric was bunched up in the back.

The woman walked down the aisle. Her dress hem dragged on the floor. The extra bows swayed side to side. She stopped next to Reverend Hagerty.

"My name is Mrs. Scott," the woman said. "Please help me. I know you are an honest Christian man."

Mrs. Scott held a small blue-velvet bag with both hands. She clutched it near her neck.

The reverend stood. "How may I assist you?" he asked.

"My husband owns a jewelry store," Mrs. Scott said. "He just got back from Chicago. He bought twenty large diamonds there. It took our life savings to buy them."

Patrick sensed Leonard's excitement over the word *diamonds*.

"Where is Mr. Scott now?" Reverend Hagerty asked.

"He had business to take care of," Mrs. Scott said. "He sent me ahead."

Suddenly she thrust her bag into Reverend Hagerty's hands. "Take the diamonds and hide them on your person," she pleaded. "Jesse James's father was a preacher. He won't rob you."

Reverend Hagerty looked stunned. "I don't think . . ."

Leonard reached over and tugged on the skirt of Mrs. Scott's dress.

She looked down at him.

"I've got a better idea," the orphan said. "Give the diamonds to me. Jesse James wouldn't rob an orphan."

Mrs. Scott's face beamed. "That *is* a better idea," she said.

Leonard quickly took the blue bag from Reverend Hagerty. "I'll keep these diamonds safe," he said. And then he grinned.

● ● ●

Beth held her breath. She could see nothing from behind the safe.

Beth thought Agent Wilson must be kneeling in front of it. She heard the soft clicks of the dial spinning.

Then she heard a pistol click. The hairs on the back of her neck stood up.

"Who's that?" the voice said. "Come out from behind the safe."

Beth tilted her head so it wasn't hidden by the iron box. She could see the bandit. And he could see her.

The man was wearing a white hood with small triangles for eyeholes. He also had on a wide-brimmed black hat. His body was covered by a thick navy-blue wool coat. His black boots reached to his knees.

Mr. Alford stood next to the robber. The conductor gave her a smile. It was meant to comfort her. But it didn't work.

Beth was too frightened. The masked man's gun was pointed at Mr. Alford.

"It's a little girl," the robber said. "The Pinkertons must have sent her. They're too scared to face me themselves."

Beth heard another man laughing. She leaned farther out and saw a second masked man.

"Which one of you is Jesse James?" she asked.

The men laughed again. They seemed like young boys at a birthday party.

"What makes you think one of us is Jesse?" the first robber said.

Beth shrugged. "I heard the James gang was bold like you," she said.

Just then Agent Wilson said, "The safe is open. Take what you want. But don't shoot the conductor."

The second masked man pushed Agent Wilson away from the safe. Then he opened a US mailbag. He stuffed the sack full with the safe's contents.

Then he picked up Agent Wilson's pistol from the table. He emptied the bullets from the weapon. He put the pistol in the bag too.

The first robber pushed Mr. Alford out the door. His gun was still pointed at the conductor.

The remaining masked man told Agent Wilson to give him his pocket watch.

Agent Wilson reached into his vest pocket. He held out the timepiece in his palm.

"It's silver," the robber said. "It isn't worth much. Keep it."

The masked man looked at Beth. He quickly reached into his pocket. He pulled out a coin and tossed it to Beth.

She snatched it out of the air with one hand. She looked at her catch. It was a silver dollar.

"Tell everyone that the bold Jesse James took a shining to you," he said. He gave her a little bow. Then suddenly he was gone.

In the Sleeper Car

The man with the bowler hat stood near the front door. He was listening intently. He said, "I hear the gang members in the passenger car."

A few seconds passed. Then the man said, "Mr. Alford is talking. He's okay."

Patrick felt like clapping. But he kept his hands still. He was glad Mr. Alford was unhurt. And he wondered what was happening to Beth and Miss Cookson and all the other orphans.

So far no gunshots had been fired. That gave Patrick hope that everyone was all right.

Reverend Hagerty stood and asked everyone to take a seat. "We'll endure this calmly. Remember, the Good Book says your money is in God's hands. If the Lord giveth, the Lord can taketh."

The men and women murmured yes and amen.

Patrick glanced at Leonard. He seemed skittish, like a cockroach after the lights come on.

"Let's go to the back," Patrick said. "We can get out that door if shooting starts."

A few moments later the front door swung open.

Mr. Alford came in first. Behind him were two very tall men. Each was wearing a white hood. Over the hoods were round black hats. The outfits looked like scarecrow costumes.

Patrick would have laughed, except for the pistols.

The pistols were small. They had silver barrels and ivory handles.

The first masked man held one in each of his hands.

Mr. Alford said to all the passengers, "Please do as these gentlemen say. No one will get hurt. Prepare to hand over your money and jewelry."

The first masked man said, "Mr. Alford is

a good example. He kindly gave me his gold pocket watch. I was very touched because it has a picture inside. It's of his father."

The masked man held up the pocket watch.

Patrick studied the man's face. The mask was tight. Patrick could see the man's long, straight nose. The first robber was Jesse James.

The second robber laughed. "The watch belonged to the conductor's dear ol' dad!" he said. "Isn't that sweet."

Anger rose up in Patrick's heart. He said, "You're mean. You shouldn't take something personal like that."

Jesse James looked directly at Patrick.

Patrick felt as if the man could read his mind.

Then Jesse's eyes shifted to Leonard.

"Well, look here, folks," Jesse James said. "Orphans. And one of them is brave." He put Mr. Alford's pocket watch into his coat pocket. "Let's search the orphans last."

The two masked men searched the adults. The robbers began with the man in the bowler hat. They found the money in his sock.

The women's purses were taken. Mrs. Scott had to give up her earrings and bracelet.

The men came to Reverend Hagerty's seat. He stood up. He held his thick wallet in his hand. He offered it to the robbers.

Jesse James said to the reverend, "Keep your wallet."

The other robber asked, "Why? Isn't his money good enough for you?"

"Look at his hands," Jesse James said. "I can tell he works for a living. They're all beat up and dirty. I want to take money only from the rich ones. They have clean, soft hands."

Finally Jesse James motioned for the boys to be searched. "You orphans," he said. "Get out of your seats. Come on up here."

Patrick stood and looked at Reverend Hagerty. The reverend nodded and smiled. His expression seemed to say, "It will be okay."

Patrick walked slowly up the aisle. He could hear Leonard shuffling behind him.

"There's a funny thing about orphans," Jesse James said. "They look poor. But they can hide all sorts of treasure."

Patrick paused. His stomach twisted like a ball of rubber bands.

"In fact," Jesse added, "there was a little orphan in the passenger car. She had nine hundred dollars hidden in her sock. I think someone gave the money to her. Maybe they thought I wouldn't search an orphan."

This guy is smart, Patrick thought.

He'll find the diamonds. Poor Mrs. Scott will lose her life savings.

Patrick was near the stove when he felt something hit his foot. Suddenly he was falling. Patrick put out his arms to catch himself. But he was too slow.

"Oof!" Patrick said. He landed on the carpet. *Leonard tripped me on purpose,* he thought.

Then Patrick felt Leonard's hand on his elbow. The orphan was helping him up.

Leonard bent down to lift Patrick. Leonard's knee hit the stove. The stove door accidentally popped open.

"Oops," Leonard said. He fumbled around with the stove door. Patrick saw a flash of something blue. Then Leonard shut the stove door.

Jesse James shouted, "That's enough fooling around. Get up here now!"

Patrick quickly stood. He moved close to the angry gang leader.

Jesse James tucked one pistol in its holster. He searched Patrick's pockets with his free hand. Right away Jesse James found the letter from Eugene. But he tossed it aside without reading it.

That was close, Patrick thought. He sighed with relief.

"Take off your boots, boy," Jesse James said. "And your socks."

Patrick took off his boots one at a time. He turned each one over and shook it. Then he peeled off his long black socks. He wiggled his bare toes.

Jesse James seemed satisfied that Patrick

had nothing of value. The man turned his attention to Leonard.

Patrick could tell all the passengers were nervous. He glanced at Mrs. Scott. She was biting her fingernails.

Reverend Hagerty's eyes were closed. His mouth was moving slightly. Patrick thought he was praying.

Leonard had already taken off his boots and socks. He stood calmly as Jesse James patted the orphan's pockets.

Any second now he's going to find those diamonds, Patrick thought.

"What is this?" Jesse James asked.

He held up something.

It was a piece of newsprint. Patrick knew it was the article about the James gang. It told about the recent stagecoach robbery.

Where are the diamonds? Patrick wondered.

Leonard beamed a smile at Jesse James. "I read all about you, sir," he said. "You're my hero!"

Leonard wrapped his arms around Jesse James and hugged him. "I want to be just like you when I grow up. Can I join your gang?"

Jesse laughed. "Of course," he said. "Come find me when you're twenty-one years old. I'll always need loyal members in my gang."

The bandit took off his hat and put it on Leonard's head.

"I'm an official member now!" Leonard said.

Jesse James stood by the front door. He said, "I had a very pleasant visit on the number seven. Thank you for your donations to the James gang."

Then Jesse reached inside his coat pocket. He handed Mr. Alford a piece of paper. "Open that when we're gone."

The second robber waved a silver-and-ivory pistol at the passengers. "Wait five minutes before you go outside. Or you'll be shot."

The robbers left out the front door.

Suddenly all the passengers began to clap. Everyone was glad the bandits were gone.

Leonard

Beth stood on top of the safe again. She looked out the vent. She counted three masked horsemen.

Then Jesse James and the other robber walked away from the train. The two men tied mailbags to their horses' saddlebags. Jesse and the second robber got on their horses.

Beth watched as each of the five bandits rode off. They all went in different directions.

They're smart, Beth thought. *Mr. Pinkerton will have five trails to follow.*

Beth jumped down from the safe. "They're gone," she said to Agent Wilson. "It's time to go see my cousin and Miss Cookson."

"Why did Jesse James give you that silver dollar?" Agent Wilson asked.

Beth had been wondering the same thing. "I think Jesse James likes children," Beth said.

"I believe you're right, miss," he said. "His favorite kind of children are spies."

Beth stomped her foot. "Do you still think I'm part of the gang?" she asked. "I told you, I did nothing wrong."

"Well," he said, "we'll still watch you. Let's go see Mr. Alford together."

Agent Wilson led Beth out the side door

of the express car. They went to the sleeper car.

The first-class passengers chattered about the robbery. One man talked about hiding his money under the carpet. He was glad the robbers hadn't found it. Reverend Hagerty was amazed that his wallet wasn't taken.

"The good Lord saw to it that my money was spared," the reverend said. "The fire darkened my hands so I looked like a laborer. Otherwise my wallet would be empty."

Mr. Alford was sitting down. He looked pale and tired.

Leonard was standing near the stove. He looked small with Jesse James's large hat on.

Patrick heard someone call his name. He turned around.

It was Beth! She moved quickly toward him.

A man followed her. He was wearing a white suit.

Miss Cookson came in from the back door. "Leonard!" she called.

Leonard rushed to her.

Miss Cookson bent over and hugged him. "I'm so grateful that you're fine," she said.

"How did you get that hat?" Miss Cookson asked.

The room suddenly fell silent. Everyone turned toward the orphan boy.

Leonard's eyes darted around the room.

The man in the bowler

hat scowled. "This young man is a fool, ma'am," he said to Miss Cookson. "He made a pact with Jesse James."

The man in the white suit shouted, "Another child spy!"

"What happened to my diamonds?" Mrs. Scott asked. She glared at Leonard. "Are *you* trying to steal them?"

Patrick didn't like the adults picking on Leonard. And it seemed Beth didn't either.

"Leonard wouldn't take your diamonds," Beth said. "But he did make a pact. It was with me. He promised not to steal."

Miss Cookson spoke up. "You should be ashamed of yourselves," she said. "Don't bully a poor orphan."

There was a short silence as everyone again looked at Leonard. He was opening the stove. He reached inside the stove with a metal scoop.

"Leonard," Miss Cookson said, "you'll get more ashes on your suit."

But Leonard didn't stop. He blew on the embers in the scoop. They glowed red. Something else was sparkling.

"Look," Leonard said, "diamonds don't burn."

"So that's why you tripped me," Patrick said. "I was so mad then. But now I get it. You had to hide the diamonds so Jesse James wouldn't find them."

Leonard nodded. "I put them in the stove," he said. "No one would look there."

Mrs. Scott said, "I'm sorry I thought you stole my diamonds. You were the bravest person on the train."

Leonard poked around in the ashes

again. He quickly picked out something white. He blew on it and put it in his pocket.

Leonard looked at Beth. "Jaguar teeth don't burn either!" he said.

Beth smiled.

Then Leonard gave Beth a sheepish grin. "I didn't steal the diamonds," he said quietly. "But I did steal something else."

Leonard reached inside his suit pocket. He pulled out a gold pocket watch. He held it up so everyone could see it.

The orphan grinned. "I think Jesse James forgot something," he said. Leonard handed the watch to Mr. Alford.

The man in the

bowler hat said, "The boy pickpocketed Jesse James! That's why he hugged him."

The people's murmurs filled the car.

Patrick said, "So you didn't want to join Jesse James's gang."

"Nope," Leonard said. "I had enough of gangs in New York."

"God bless you, boy," Mr. Alford said. There were tears in the man's eyes. "My father's watch. How can I ever thank you?"

"You can let me and the other orphans stay in first class," Leonard said.

The End of the Line

Beth and Patrick sat together in first-class seats near the front of the car. She told Patrick everything that had happened to her. And he told her about the robbery in the first-class car.

Jesse James had stolen everything valuable in the express car. So Agent Wilson had nothing to guard. Mr. Alford let Agent Wilson stay in the first-class section too.

Beth whispered to Patrick, "Is Agent Wilson watching me?"

Patrick looked over his shoulder for a moment. "Yes," he whispered. "Maybe he thinks you're going to jump out the window."

The train whistled three times. The bell rang. The Iron Mountain Express number 7 moved away from the Gad's Hill station.

Mr. Alford checked his pocket watch. Then he came to punch their tickets. Beth and Patrick each handed him their tickets.

"Remember the paper Jesse James gave you?" Patrick asked the conductor.

Mr. Alford nodded.

"What did it say?" Patrick asked.

Mr. Alford chuckled. "It was a summary of the robbery for the newspapers."

"A press release?" Beth asked.

"Yes," Mr. Alford said. "I can't show it to you. It's evidence now. But the headline was 'The Most Daring Robbery on Record.'"

Beth giggled. She said, "I think it should have said, 'Daring Orphan Saves Diamonds.'"

Mr. Alford leaned forward. He said in hushed tones, "Mrs. Scott is going to pay for Leonard to go to boarding school."

"But he needs parents," Beth said, "not just an education."

Mr. Alford patted Beth on the shoulder. "That's what Miss Cookson said too. Reverend Hagerty plans to look for homes for all the orphans. He hopes to find the right home for Leonard. Some Christian couple will have a great son."

"If his new parents can keep him out of trouble," Patrick added. He motioned with his head.

Beth looked in that direction.

Reverend Hagerty was asleep. His head was tilted back in the seat. His chest rose and fell with each snore.

Leonard stood next to him. He was braiding the reverend's beard!

● ● ●

The train finally stopped at Little Rock, Arkansas. It was dawn.

Patrick looked out the window. He nudged Beth.

"Is that Mr. Pinkerton?" he asked.

A man was on the platform. He had a white shirt on. And he was scowling.

"Yes," Beth said. "That's the famous detective."

Mr. Alford came through the first-class section.

"Everyone off the train," the conductor said. "This is the end of the line."

Miss Cookson gathered all the orphans on the train platform. Patrick and Beth waited with the group.

Patrick watched as Mr. Pinkerton and Agent Wilson spoke.

Patrick asked Beth, "What do you think they're talking about?"

"Us," Beth said. "They're coming our way."

The detective and the agent moved toward the orphans. But the men didn't talk to the cousins. Mr. Pinkerton went straight to Miss Cookson.

Whatever the detective said made

Miss Cookson smile. She rushed to Patrick and Beth.

"This is glorious news!" she said. "Detective Pinkerton has found your guardian."

Patrick glanced at Beth. She was pale. Her hands were shaking.

"Guardian?" Patrick said.

"Yes!" Miss Cookson said. "A man named Eugene. I'm surprised you didn't tell me about him."

Miss Cookson kissed Beth on the cheeks. "Farewell, my dear," she said. "Remember to be on time."

Miss Cookson took Patrick's hand and leaned in close. She whispered in his ear, "I knew you didn't take the apple."

The kind woman bid farewell again. Then she gathered the orphans and herded them off the train platform.

Patrick closed his eyes. He prayed a little prayer. He asked God to find good homes for the children.

Patrick opened his eyes. Mr. Pinkerton and Agent Wilson were standing in front of him.

Agent Wilson said, "We found this on the floor of the sleeper car." He held up an envelope. "We need to go to the courthouse so you can explain a few things."

It was Eugene's letter with the name Patrick clearly written on it.

We're doomed, Patrick thought.

Jail

Mr. Pinkerton and Agent Wilson walked behind Beth and Patrick. They were all headed to a white building. A sign on it said County Courthouse.

Beth knew that's where the jail was. Her stomach burned with worry. It felt as if she'd sipped a cup of bleach.

"Why didn't Eugene come to meet us at the depot?" Patrick asked.

Agent Wilson glanced at Mr. Pinkerton. They shared a knowing look.

"You'll see Eugene soon enough," Mr. Pinkerton said. "And we'll sort out your future."

Future? Beth didn't want to spend her future in jail.

The courthouse was a two-story, wood building. It had red trim and four steps leading to the front door.

Beth's boots felt like lead as she plodded up each step.

Mr. Pinkerton opened the double doors. All four of them walked through. Agent Wilson led the way.

They passed hallways that had portraits on the walls. The men in the paintings seemed to frown on Beth.

The group passed offices with desks. They came to the back of the building.

"Follow the stairs," Mr. Pinkerton said. "Eugene is waiting. Agent Wilson and I have to talk to the court recorder."

Beth and Patrick walked down a few steps.

Beth saw what she dreaded. Iron bars. Cement walls.

Eugene was in one of the cells. He was sitting on a small cot with a gray blanket. A Bible was on a nearby table. He seemed lonely. But otherwise he looked okay.

Patrick called, "Eugene!"

Eugene looked surprised. "Patrick!" he said. "Beth!" Then he jumped up. "Did you see him?"

Beth moved toward the cell.

Patrick was confused. "See who? Mr. Whittaker?"

It was Eugene's turn to look confused. "I haven't thought about him," he said. "I was referring to Jesse James."

Beth moved closer to the bars. "Oh, him," Beth said. She sounded defeated.

"Yes, him!" Eugene said. "The master criminal has eluded some of the best detectives in history! I was hot on his trail."

"Until you got arrested," Patrick said.

Suddenly a bright light filled the jail cell.

The car Imagination Station appeared just as Mr. Pinkerton and Agent Wilson entered. Only Beth, Patrick, and Eugene could see the Station.

Patrick realized the problem at once. He and Beth couldn't get inside the cell to reach the machine.

Beth must have realized the problem

too. She turned to Mr. Pinkerton. "I insist that you arrest us," she said. "I confess to knowing more about Jesse James than you do."

The detective took off his hat. His eyebrows scrunched. "I can't arrest you for that," he said. "I didn't listen when you warned me."

Beth reached inside her pocket. She showed the silver dollar to Agent Wilson. "Do you remember this?"

The agent nodded. "Jesse James gave that to you."

Beth said, "And would you say it was probably stolen?"

Again the agent nodded.

"Then I'm in possession of stolen goods," Beth said. "Arrest us!"

Mr. Pinkerton took a key out of the inside

of his coat. He put the key in the lock and turned it. The door clicked.

Patrick and Beth rushed inside the cell.

"Hurry," Patrick said. "Get in the machine. What are you waiting for, Eugene?"

He looked at his friend. Eugene still looked glum.

"Your plan has a flaw," Eugene said. "There are only two seats in this machine."

"So one of us has to stay behind," Beth said. It was a fact. Not a question.

Patrick heard a click. He turned.

Mr. Pinkerton had locked all three of them inside the cell.

**Find out what happens next in
adventure 19,
*Light in the Lions' Den.***

Secret Word Puzzle

Railroads like to keep their trains on time. Station agents and conductors check their watches often. They want to make sure the train stops are on schedule. In the 1870s, many railroad officials used pocket watches. And those pocket watches had Roman numerals on them.

Roman Numeral Key

I	= 1	V	= 5	IX	= 9
II	= 2	VI	= 6	X	= 10
III	= 3	VII	= 7	XI	= 11
IV	= 4	VIII	= 8	XII	= 12

Use this clock to break the following math code. Each Roman numeral on the clock corresponds to a letter. Fill in the letters on the blanks. Then you'll know part of James 1:27. (The last word in the code is the secret word.)

$$\frac{L}{3+3} \quad \frac{O}{4+4} \quad \frac{O}{10-2} \quad \frac{K}{1+4} \qquad \frac{A}{3-2} \quad \frac{F}{6-3} \quad \frac{T}{10+2} \quad \frac{E}{5-3} \quad \frac{R}{5+5}$$

$$\frac{O}{9-1} \quad \frac{R}{6+4} \quad \frac{P}{8+1} \quad \frac{H}{2+2} \quad \frac{A}{6-5} \quad \frac{N}{9-2} \quad \frac{S}{5+6}$$

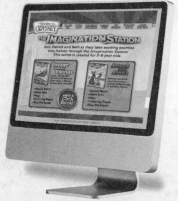

*Go to **TheImaginationStation.com**.
Find the cover of this book.
Click on "Secret Word."
Type in the answer,
and you'll receive a prize.*